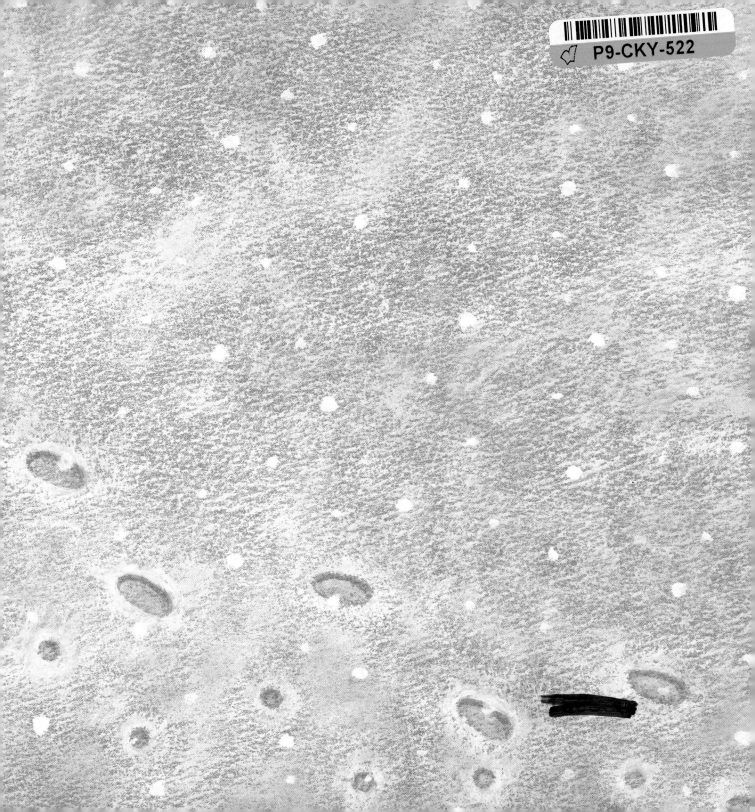

Under My Hood

BY **KARLA KUSKIN**

ILLUSTRATED BY **FUMI KOSAKA**

LAURA GERINGER BOOKS
An Imprint of HarperCollinsPublishers

I Have a Hat

Under my hood

I have a hat

and under that

my hair is flat.

Under my coat

my sweater's blue.

My sweater's red.
I'm wearing two.

My muffler

muffles to my chin
and round my neck
and then tucks in.

My gloves were knitted
by my aunts.

I've mittens too

and pants
and pants

and boots
and shoes
with socks inside.
The boots are rubber, red and wide.

And when I walk

I must not fall

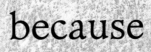

because

I can't get up at all.